Three Rapping Rats

Making music with traditional stories

by Kaye Umansky

with ideas for musical development by
Stephen Chadwick and Kate Buchanan
and illustrations by Dee Shulman

'DRAWN

cover illustration by Alex Ayliffe

A & C Black • London

First published 1998 by A & C Black (Publishers) Ltd
35 Bedford Row, London WC1R 4JH

Story text © Kaye Umansky
Teacher's notes for *King Midas, Sleeping Beauty, The Island of Plums, Henry VIII's Proposal, Rumpelstiltskin* and *Mowgli in the Jungle* by Kate Buchanan; *The Sun and Wind, The Princess and the Pea, Stone Soup, Imir the Frost Giant* and *The Pied Piper* by Stephen Chadwick © A & C Black

Illustrations by Dee Shulman
Cover illustration by Alex Ayliffe
Designed by Dorothy Moir
Edited by Ana Sanderson

Printed in Great Britain by St Edmundsbury Press Ltd, Bury St Edmunds, Suffolk

The authors and publisher would like to thank the following for their help during the preparation of this book:
Marney Duncan, Sarah Farr, Audrey Mason, Sheena Roberts, Jane Sebba and Elaine Sutton.

Contents

Introduction

Three Rapping Rats is the sequel to **Three Singing Pigs**. It is full of excellent stories and musical activities for older children to inspire them to perform and compose. Everyone can use this book – whether they have a musical training or have never read a note of music in their lives. This is how the book works.

Each story contains inherent musical elements. For instance, in *Sleeping Beauty*, everything around the princess slows down to a stop (tempo); in *The Pied Piper*, there is a hypnotic melody (pitch). The stories have been told with these elements in mind, and each is followed by clear instructions which show you how to build the story into your music lessons.

In most cases, two activities are suggested – a short activity and a longer one. The short activities are designed to be used with little preparation. The longer activities explore musical ideas more thoroughly, and build up to a more advanced performance. You may need to find instruments or photocopy an illustration beforehand. You will also need to do more preparation with the children – for instance, there may be a musical game to play, sounds to explore, or an accompaniment to practise. Don't try to achieve too much in one lesson – spread the preparation over two or more sessions.

The stories work through the elements of music and a degree of progression is built into the book. No one need feel compelled to start at the beginning and work all the way through. However, if you do, you will find yourself starting with duration (keeping a steady pulse) and ending with pitch (higher and lower sounds). The musical elements which are the main focus are listed with the stories on the contents page.

Musical instruments

There is plenty of scope for you to use any tuned and untuned percussion instruments you may have available. Don't be put off if your music cupboard is not well stocked with multiple sets of maracas, woodblocks, tambours etc. There are many suggestions for sound-makers and 'junk' instruments you can find around the home or the classroom. If you wish to develop your collection of percussion instruments, a useful directory to refer to is **Agogo bells to xylophone** by Maggie Cotton (published by A & C Black).

Using a score

A score is simply a means of showing musicians when and how to play. It might be written in musical notation like the score of a Beethoven symphony, or it might be a picture – like the spinning wheel on page 37. Picture scores are used frequently in this book – some, like the spinning wheel score, tell the children when to play notes, others are less precise. Some scores are pictures which can be interpreted in a variety of ways, as the instructions explain. All the scores in this book may be photocopied. Enlarge them and paste them on to card for re-use.

The songs

All the songs and raps in this book can be taught by rote. To aid teaching, you can, if you wish, handwrite the words on to an overhead projector sheet for the children to see. The songs in this book consist of new words set to well-known tunes. The melody lines are given with guitar chords at the back of the book; if you don't know a tune, ask a music reader to play it for you.

Making the most of the stories

The stories can be put to work in a variety of ways. They can be related to topics or cross-curricular work, e.g. *Imir the Frost Giant* is a Viking story, *Henry VIII's Proposal* relates to Tudor history, *The Sun and Wind* to science and geography. The stories can be presented in assembly or at end-of-term performances. They can be developed dramatically: dialogue improvised, parts acted out, and dance and mime included. Masks, simple costumes and props can be made with the children's help. In short, the stories can do as much or as little as you want them to. Take them and enjoy them with your children!

King Midas

This song (which is sung to the tune of *I Came From Alabama*) tells the story of the Greek myth about King Midas. It is performed with a chanted call and response introduction to each verse (short activity) and with ostinato accompaniments played on untuned percussion (longer activity).

Gonna tell you all the story
Of a wealthy king of old, * *
With an overriding passion
For collecting lots of gold. * *
And he stored it in his cellar
Where you couldn't shut the door, * *
But it never was enough for him,
He always wanted more. * *

   Oh, King Midas,
   'Cos greed's your middle name, * *
   You are sure to come a cropper,
   Which will be an awful shame! * *

Well, the god named Dionysus
Came to Midas late one night, * *
'Gonna let you make a wish, my friend,
Be sure and get it right.' * *
'Tell you what,' said greedy Midas,
'If I might just be so bold, * *
Could you make it so that everything
I touch will turn to gold?' * *

   Oh, King Midas,
   'Cos greed's your middle name, * *
   You are sure to come a cropper,
   Which will be an awful shame! * *

Well, he touched the kitchen table
And he touched the kitchen door, * *
And he left great golden footprints
Right across the kitchen floor. * *
Then he raced around the palace
Just as happy as can be, * *
But he knew he was in trouble
When he sat down for his tea! * *

   Oh, King Midas,
   'Cos greed's your middle name, * *
   You are sure to come a cropper,
   Which will be an awful shame! * *

It was then that old King Midas
Got himself into a state, * *
Because everything he handled
Turned to gold upon his plate. * *
What's the moral of this story?
What's the lesson in this song? * *
If you try to be too greedy
Things will always turn out wrong! * *

   Oh, King Midas,
   'Cos greed's your middle name, * *
   You are sure to come a cropper,
   Which will be an awful shame! * *

Short activity

The children learn the song. Then they learn a call and response chant using words from the song. The call and response is performed as an introduction to each verse.

The song

1. Either teach everyone all four verses of the song, or divide the children into four groups and teach one verse of the song to each. Each verse starts on the note D. Play it on a piano or tuned percussion instrument before you start.

When teaching the song, sing two lines and ask the children to echo; sing the next two lines and so on. If you can, avoid taking a breath between pairs of lines.

Where there is a pair of asterisks, clap twice, in time with the beat of the song.

2. Teach everyone the chorus. It starts on the note G. Then try performing the whole song.

A call and response chant

1. Chant these words in the rhythm with which you would sing them:

Gonna tell you all

Then chant the following extended version with a strong rhythm:

**Gonna tell you all,
Gonna tell you all,
Gonna tell, gonna tell,
Gonna tell you all.**

2. The *Gonna Tell You All* chant is shown in the box below as a call and response for soloist and group. Try chanting it with volunteer soloists. If you wish, the children can clap on the words *you all*.

3. When the call and response chant is secure, try a performance of the whole song. Perform the call and response chant as an introduction to each verse.

Gonna Tell You All –
Call and response chant

| Gon-na tell | *you* *all,* | Gon-na tell | *you* *all,* | Gon-na tell, | gon-na tell, | Gon-na tell | *you* *all.* |
| 1 | 2 | 3 | 4 | 1 | 2 | 3 | 4 |

Longer activity

The children play ostinato patterns on untuned percussion instruments. These are used as an accompaniment to the song.

What you will need

* Untuned percussion instruments – a drum, a cymbal and a tambourine
* Enlarged photocopies of the ostinato boxes below

Preparation

1. Divide into two groups. One sings the song while the other quietly performs the *Gonna Tell You All* chant at the same time, over and over again.

2. Choose three children from the *Gonna Tell You All* group to play instruments – drum, cymbal and tambourine. Allocate to each a photocopy of the ostinato patterns below. Explain that:
• the drum is played on the word *tell*;
• the cymbal is played on the word *all*;
• the tambourine is played on the words *you all*.

3. Practise each pattern separately with, then without, the *Gonna Tell You All* chant. When the three players can perform confidently, combine different pairs of instruments, e.g. drum and cymbals, drum and tambourine. Then play all the ostinato patterns at the same time.

Performance

Sing the song. Include the *Gonna Tell You All* chant as an introduction and link between verses. Accompany the song with the instrumental patterns. Decide which pattern is best suited for which verse; finish with all three patterns played together to accompany verse 4.

Ostinato accompaniment patterns

Drum pattern – play on 'tell'

Gon-na tell   you   all,   Gon-na tell   you   all,   Gon-na tell,   gon-na tell,   Gon-na tell   you   all.

Cymbal pattern – play on 'all'

Gon-na tell   you   all,   Gon-na tell   you   all,   Gon-na tell,   gon-na tell,   Gon-na tell   you   all.

Tambourine pattern – play on 'you all'

Gon-na tell   you   all,   Gon-na tell   you   all,   Gon-na tell,   gon-na tell,   Gon-na tell   you   all.

Sleeping Beauty

The story is told in narrative and song (sung to the tune of *On Top of Old Smokey*). The children explore getting slower and faster with sound effects (short activity) and make up pieces which get slower and faster representing the soldiers, birds and clocks (longer activities).

They say there's a castle
On a mountain so steep,
Inside lies a princess
Who's forever asleep.
They say she liked dancing,
In a blue satin gown,
Then she pricked her finger,
(Getting slower)
And ... time ... slowed ... right ... down.

Everything around the princess slowed right down. The soldiers who had been marching in the courtyard ... the birds, which had been singing in the garden ... even the clocks ... everyone and everything slowed right down.

(SOLDIERS MUSIC, getting slower)
(BIRDS MUSIC, getting slower)
(CLOCKS MUSIC, getting slower)

Everyone fell into an enchanted sleep – and in the palace, time stood still for a hundred years. During that time, thorny hedges grew and surrounded the castle and bramble bushes became as thick as walls. Small saplings grew into tall trees. Finally, all that could be seen of the castle from the outside was the golden weather vane on the top of the tallest tower. And then ...

A prince came a-riding,
From a faraway land,
He entered the forest
With a sword in his hand,
Through thorns and through brambles
He fought with a will,
And entered the castle
Where ... time ... had ... stood ... still.

And there, the prince saw a strange sight. Everybody was asleep. The soldiers, the kitchen staff, the gardeners ... everybody.

Slowly, the prince moved through the enchanted castle until he came to a flight of stairs. Up, up he climbed – and at the top he found a bedchamber. Pushing aside the cobwebs, he went in – and there lay the sleeping princess. Quite overcome by her loveliness, the prince knelt beside her and tenderly kissed her cheek. The princess stirred and opened her eyes. And everyone else in the castle woke at the same time. The soldiers in the courtyard began to march ... the birds in the garden began to sing ... and the clocks began to tick.

(SOLDIERS MUSIC, getting faster)
(BIRDS MUSIC, getting faster)
(CLOCKS MUSIC, getting faster)

At last it is over,
Again all is well,
No more is the princess
Lying under a spell,
Again she is dancing
In her blue satin gown,
The days are forgotten
When ... time ... slowed ... right ... down.

9

Short activity

In this version, vocal and body sounds which get slower or faster are added to the narrative. The children also sing the song.

1. Play *Shadow Me* (page 13), a game in which the children copy a leader who gets faster or slower.

2. Think of vocal and body sounds for the soldiers, birds and clocks in the story. Here are some suggestions:

birds singing

soldiers marching

clocks ticking

3. Choose six leaders (one each to direct the soldiers, birds and clocks in the 'getting slower', and in the 'getting faster' versions). As in the *Shadow Me* game, the rest of the children 'shadow' each leader while making the appropriate sound effect.

4. Teach the song. Play C on a piano or tuned percussion instrument for your starting note. Get slower when singing the last line of each verse.

5. When the song and the 'getting slower' and 'getting faster' sounds are well established, perform the whole story. The vocal and body sounds should last long enough to demonstrate the changing pace. For the 'getting faster' sounds, start very slowly and finish at a medium, realistic pace.

Longer activities

In this section, there are suggestions for making up music for the soldiers, the birds and the clocks. The pieces explore gradually getting slower and faster. Explore the activities with the whole class before dividing the children into groups for the performance.

Soldiers Music

The children imitate soldiers marching by alternating left and right knee taps, chanting the words *left right* and playing a drum accompaniment. The change of tempo is controlled by a leader who is shadowed (as in the *Shadow Me* game) by the other children.

What you will need

* Four or five drums and pairs of beaters

Preparation – getting slower

1. Everyone chants these words at a moderate speed, tapping their left and right knees alternately.

Left   right   left   right   left   right ...

2. Choose a child to be the leader. The other children shadow the leader (as they did in *Shadow Me*) as (s)he performs the words and knee taps, gradually getting slower.

Left   right   left ...   right ...   left ...

3. Choose some children to play the drums. Give each child a pair of beaters. Teach them this pattern:

(Spoken)
Left   right   left   right   left   right   left   right ...

4. Organise your performance. The leader indicates to the children to begin the chant, the knee taps and the drum beats at the marching pace. The children then carefully 'shadow' the leader who gradually slows the pace down to a stop.

Getting faster

The leader indicates to the children to chant, tap and drum at a very slow pace, using arm gestures. (If the leader wishes, the drummer can begin later.) Everyone carefully shadows the leader who gradually increases the pace to a good marching pace, but no faster. Work out an effective ending to the piece (e.g. choose one drummer to decide when to make a big 'stop' gesture on the final drum strike).

Birds Music

The children divide into groups to make up music which imitates bird calls. The groups follow a conductor's signals to begin, get faster, get slower and stop.

Bird Call Pictures

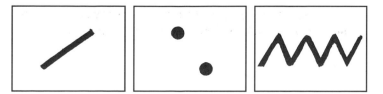

What you will need

* A variety of tuned instruments, e.g. recorders, swanee whistles, glockenspiels and so on

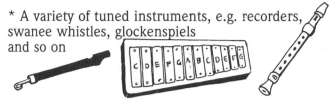

* Enlarged photocopies of the bird call pictures
* Several long pieces of paper, and pencils

Preparation – getting slower

1. Show the children the bird call pictures and ask them to describe the differences between them (e.g. one slides from low to high; one consists of two short sounds – one high, the other low; one wiggles up and down).

2. Divide the children into small groups, allocating pitched instruments to each. Each group makes up vocal and instrumental bird call sounds for each picture. If they wish, the children can make up new bird calls and draw pictures for them.

3. Each group makes up *Birds Music* by thinking of sequences of bird calls. Each group then draws their sequence of bird calls on long pieces of paper. Here is an example sequence:

4. Choose a child to conduct a performance of the *Birds Music*. The conductor will:
• signal to all the groups to begin playing together;
• signal when the music should start gradually slowing down;
• signal to groups or performers when to drop out or stop.
To do this, the conductor will need to agree gestures to use as signals with the groups.

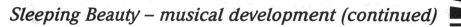
Getting faster

The conductor:
• signals to the groups one at a time to begin playing very slowly;
• signals when the music should get gradually faster;
• signals when to stop.

Clocks Music

The children perform three *tick tock* patterns which fit together. One is fast, one is medium-speed and one is slow. The effect of slowing down in the music is achieved by the fast and medium *tick tock* patterns dropping out – leaving the slow pattern.

What you will need

* A drum
* Three groups of instruments to imitate the sound of a clock, e.g. claves, two tone woodblocks and guiros.

Preparation – getting slower

1. The children stand in a circle. They will perform one at a time, passing patterns around the circle, in time with a drum beat.

2. Play a steady drum beat. The children perform the first *tick tock* pattern. The first child says *tick-tock* on the first beat, second child says *tick-tock* on the second beat, third child says (or thinks) *rest* on the third beat and so on. Whenever a child says (or thinks) the word *rest*, (s)he sits down and is out. The pattern is continued until all the children in the circle are sitting down.

3. Try the same process with the other two patterns. (Notice that in the third pattern, the second child, fourth child, sixth child and so on make a silent gesture – putting their hands over their mouths.)

4. Divide the children into three equal groups – one for each pattern. The groups perform the patterns simultaneously with a steady drum beat. The three groups start their patterns together – the first group will finish first, followed by the second, then the third.

5. Repeat stage 4 without the steady drum beat. The groups must maintain a steady beat by listening to each other. What is the overall effect without the drum beat? (It sounds as though the music gets slower although the beat is constant.)

6. Add instruments. Play the three patterns on untuned percussion instruments. Ask the children which instruments would be appropriate for each pattern (e.g. claves for the first pattern, two tone woodblocks for the second, and guiros for the third).

1st tick tock pattern – fast

2nd tick tock pattern – medium

3rd tick tock pattern – slow

Clocks music – three groups performing simultaneously

Group 1 performing the fast pattern

Group 2 performing the medium pattern

Group 3 performing the slow pattern

Getting faster

Choose a child to conduct. The conductor indicates to the third group, then the second group, then the first group to perform so that they are all performing together. The children do not sit down on the word *rest*. Ask the conductor to decide how the piece should end (e.g. at a moment when children in all three groups are silent simultaneously).

Performance

Tell the story, incorporating the song and performances of the six pieces of music. Divide the children into appropriately sized groups for the six pieces; you will probably need more children for the clocks groups than for the soldiers or birds groups.

Shadow Me

In this game, the children practise following a leader who directs the change of pace. The leader gets faster or slower and the children copy. This game requires everyone's attention and concentration.

Choose an action, such as clapping (or knee tapping, stamping, finger clicking and so on). Perform your chosen sound with a steady beat. Ask the children to copy you as you make your sound – as though they are your shadow.

Try getting gradually slower. Are the children getting slower with you? Gradually get faster. Are the children getting faster with you? Try not to get louder or quieter as you gradually change the pace.

Choose a child to be the leader. (S)he can perform a different action for the other children to shadow.

The Island of Plums

This story is told in narrative and song. The children sing the song to the tune of *Shortnin' Bread*, exploring different tempos and dynamics (short activity). They make up journey music, and learn accompaniment parts for the song (longer activities).

Brer Buzzard was busy selling his plums in the market. He sang (to the tune of *Shortnin' Bread*):

Nice ripe plums! Nice ripe plums!
Nothing like the taste of nice ripe plums!
What a treat for empty tums!
Nothing like the taste of nice ripe plums!
    Come and get your plums here,
    Plump, round, yellow ones,
    Big, sweet, purple ones,
    Nice, ripe plums!

Anansi the Spider stood at the back of the crowd, watching Brer Buzzard get rich. Plums were a rare treat on Animal Island. He wondered where they came from. In front of Anansi stood his old enemies, Brer Rabbit and Brer Bear. Brer Rabbit was urgently singing in a whisper into Brer Bear's ear:

Don't let on! Don't you tell!
I know where he gets those plums to sell!
Every morn at break of day,
He stretches out his wings and flies away.
    Flyin' to an island,
    Secret island,
    Flyin' to an island
    Far away.

Just after dawn, Brer Buzzard flew off. Straight away, Brer Bear and Brer Rabbit cast off in their boat and sailed away with the morning breeze. And right behind them came Anansi!

(1ST JOURNEY MUSIC)

Before long, Plum Island loomed ahead. The moment Brer Bear and Brer Rabbit landed, they went rushing off to pick plums. They went plum crazy. They rushed from tree to tree, stuffing themselves while singing excitedly:

Grab those plums! Stuff them in!
Let the sticky juice drip down your chin!
Nice ripe plums! Eat them quick!
Gobble all the plums up 'til you're sick.
    Gobble all the plums up,
    Big, sweet, purple plums,
    Gobble all the plums up
    'Til you're sick!

Oh dear no! What a blow!
Simply can't believe I've got to row,
Out of breath, tired and hot,
Wonder if I'll make it? I think not.
    Think I'm getting slower,
    I'm no rower,
    Wonder if I'll make it?
    I – think – not.

When Anansi arrived, he didn't waste time eating the plums. Instead, he began to fill his boat up, slowly and methodically. It wasn't long before Brer Bear and Brer Rabbit spotted him climbing up a plum tree with his sack. It was then that they decided to play a mean trick. They sneaked along to his boat and stole his sail! Then they pushed out their own boat and headed for home. When Anansi arrived back at his boat, he was horrified to find his sail had vanished.

Just then, Brer Alligator stuck his head over the side. 'Hey there, Anansi. What are you doing all alone in the middle of the sea?' he asked curiously.

'Rowing my plums to the mainland,' said Anansi.

'They'll be rotten by the time you get there,' observed Brer Alligator.

'Want a bet?' said Anansi. 'I'll get there before you can count to a hundred.'

'Ha!' said Brer Alligator. 'I can get there by the time you can count to fifty.'

'I know!' said crafty Anansi. 'Let's work together. You pull, I'll row. Let's see if we can do it by twenty-five.'

'Agreed,' said Brer Alligator, and he grabbed

There was nothing for it but to row home. It would take days – and all his plums would go rotten. What a disaster. And he sang (getting slower and slower):

the boat's rope and set off at the speed of light.

(2ND JOURNEY MUSIC)

As the boat scudded over the waves, Anansi couldn't help feeling very pleased with himself! And he sang (triumphantly):

Hoot that horn! Bang those drums!
I'm a-comin' home with all my plums!
Hip hooray! What a day!
Once again Anansi gets his way!
    Clever old spider,
    What a spider,
    Trust Anansi to
    Get his way!

As for Brer Rabbit and Brer Bear – well, the extra sail didn't do them any good at all. The wind had changed direction, and kept blowing them back to the island, where they had to stay for weeks and weeks, living on plums. And they sang (painfully):

We've been tricked! We've been had!
Can't remember feeling quite this bad.
Oooh my head! Oooh my tum!
Never want to see another plum.
    Liked 'em when we ate 'em,
    Now we hate 'em,
    Can't face eatin'
    Another plum.

Meanwhile, in the market, Anansi was busily selling his plums for a huge profit, and singing (loudly and vigorously):

Nice ripe plums! Nice ripe plums!
Nothing like the taste of nice ripe plums!
What a treat for empty tums!
Nothing like the taste of nice ripe plums!
    Come and get your plums here,
    Plump, round, yellow ones,
    Big, sweet, purple ones,
    Nice, ripe plums!

Short activity

The children sing the verses of the song, paying special attention to tempo and dynamics. The song begins on the note C'.

1. Discuss with the children the different characters in the story and what happens to them. Use the pictures below if you wish.

2. Consider how each character might sing his verses – quickly, slowly or in between; loudly, quietly or in between. Ask the children to invent actions (e.g. rub tummy for *What a treat for empty tums*; stretch out arms as if flying for *He stretches out his wings and flies away*, and so on).

3. Read the story again, singing the verses of the song appropriately for each character.

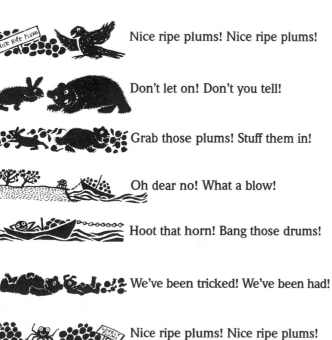

Nice ripe plums! Nice ripe plums!

Don't let on! Don't you tell!

Grab those plums! Stuff them in!

Oh dear no! What a blow!

Hoot that horn! Bang those drums!

We've been tricked! We've been had!

Nice ripe plums! Nice ripe plums!

Longer activities

The children make up music for both Anansi's journeys, using two different tempos. They also learn accompaniment parts for the song.

Journey Music

What you will need

* A selection of untuned percussion instruments, e.g.

Preparation for 1st Journey Music

Anansi's journey to the Island of Plums is rather leisurely – his sails catch the gentle morning breeze.

1. Chant the words *sailed away with the morning breeze* with a slow, lilting rhythm. Ask pairs of children to choose different untuned percussion instruments which have light, gentle sounds (e.g. maracas, triangle) to play with the words:

sailed	a - way with the morn	- ing breeze

2. Chant the words twice and create a longer sequence, (e.g. use more instruments):

sailed	a - way with the morn	- ing breeze

sailed	a - way with the morn	- ing breeze

3. Discuss the dynamics of this sequence in relation to the story. What would the effect be of the boat going off into the distance? (The sound would get quieter and quieter). Discuss how this could be shown in the music. (The voices and instruments could drop out one at a time, or the voices could stop altogether leaving the instruments to fade out.)

4. Ask the children to decide how many times to repeat the chant for the performance, what instruments they will use and when they will get quieter.

Preparation for 2nd Journey Music

Anansi is towed back very quickly by Brer Alligator.

1. The children say these words and clap their rhythm, emphasizing the first and last words:

Set　off　at　the　speed　of　**light**

2. Sit in a circle to play this rhythm game. One child says the phrase and as (s)he says the word *light*, the next child starts the phrase with the word *set*. The pattern is continued. How fast can the children pass the phrase round the circle?

3. Divide the children into two or three groups. Perform stage 2 with contrasting drum sounds (e.g. group 1 – skin – bongos or tambours; group 2 –

wooden – slit or gato drums, and so on). Play the rhythms quickly and loudly, but with a light touch.

4. Ask the children to decide how many times to repeat the phrase, what instruments they will use and whether it is appropriate to change dynamics in the performance.

Song accompaniment

The song begins on the note C' and uses these notes:

This combination of notes is called a pentatonic scale.

What you will need

* as many tuned instruments (e.g. chime bars, glockenspiels, xylophones, keyboards) with the notes C and G, and C D and E as you have available

* untuned percussion instruments

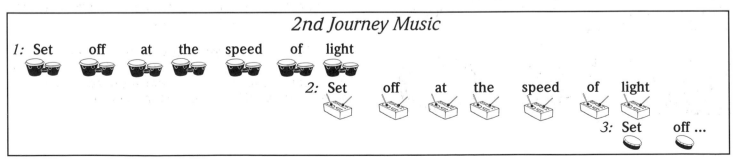

2nd Journey Music

1: Set　off　at　the　speed　of　light

2: Set　off　at　the　speed　of　light

3: Set　off ...

Tuned Accompaniment Part 1

1. Sing Brer Buzzard's version of the song. On the words *Nice ripe plums* at the end of the second, fourth and eighth lines, tap your knees three times.

2. Silently 'sing' the song in your head tapping at the correct moments.

3. Sing the other verses, playing the notes E D C instead of tapping. They are the same as the tune.

Tuned Accompaniment Part 2

1. Choose any word rhythm from the song (e.g. *Nice ripe plums*; or *Plump, round yellow ones*, and so on). Choose some children to clap it over and over again throughout the song as the others sing it.

2. Play the word rhythm using the notes C and G in any order. (Use the lowest Cs and Gs you have available.) Sing the song again, playing the pattern throughout.

Untuned Accompaniment Parts

The children can play word rhythms on untuned percussion. They can also think of sounds effects, (e.g. a wind effect for sailing).

Combining the accompaniment parts

The children play the tuned accompaniment parts 1 and 2, and untuned accompaniments, at the same time.

1. Encourage the children to practise playing at different tempos and dynamics.

2. Try out different combinations of instruments to create a variety of textures, e.g. xylophones of different sizes, metallophones only, xylophones playing the low pattern with glockenspiels and chime bars playing higher E D C pattern. Experiment with the different sound effects on keyboards and write down the number which has to be programmed in (e.g. 23 = electric bass; 14 = piano).

3. Read the story and, with the children, decide which of the combinations of instruments, and what tempo and dynamics, are appropriate for each of the seven verses of the song. (Note that the words of song verses 1 and 7 are the same.)

Performance

To tell the story, and play the different song accompaniments and *1st* and *2nd Journey Music*, you may wish to divide the children into nine groups, allocating a section of music to each. You can place the groups in a horseshoe shape in the order in which they play. Alternatively, write down which children perform at each stage and what they play.

(Note that the *1st Journey Music* gets gradually quieter over a number of repetitions. If you wish, the story can be continued over the music, which can get louder at the point when 'Plum Island' looms ahead.)

The Sun and Wind

This story is told in narrative and song. The Wind's song is sung to the tune of *This Old Man*. The Sun's song is sung to the tune of *Michael Finnigin*. The children sing the songs and make sounds at different dynamics to convey the increasing strength of the sun and wind (short activities). They then sing the songs simultaneously as partner songs and use instruments for the sun and wind music (longer activities).

The Wind had been in a bad temper all week. It had blown down trees, had stamped on a cornfield – and had even blown the roof off a farmhouse. It was feeling so grumpy that it decided to pick an argument with the Sun. It began by singing a very boastful song (*This Old Man*):

> I'm the Wind! I am strong!
> I can blow the clouds along!
> Gonna pinch your kite and
>   throw it in a tree,
> No one is as strong as me!

And the Wind blew a light air force 1.

(1ST WIND BLOWING MUSIC, p)

'That's nothing,' said the Sun. 'I can do better than that.' And it sang (*Michael Finnigin*):

> It's holiday time for everyone again,
> Time to swim and jump and run again,
> Take your coat off, here's the sun again,
> Summer has begun again! It's fun again!

And the Sun shone 10 degrees celsius lukewarm.

(1ST SUN SHINING MUSIC, p)

'Pathetic,' scoffed the Wind. 'Watch this.'

> I'm the wind! I am strong!
> I can blow the clouds along!
> Gonna pinch your hat and
>   blow it out to sea,
> No one is as strong as me!

And the Wind blew a strong breeze force 6.

(2ND WIND BLOWING MUSIC, mf)

'Not bad,' said the Sun. 'But watch this.'

> It's holiday time for everyone again,
> Time to swim and jump and run again,
> Take your shoes off, here's the sun again,
> Summer has begun again! It's fun again!

And the Sun shone 30 degrees celsius baking hot.

(2ND SUN SHINING MUSIC, mf)

'Feeble,' mocked the Wind. 'Watch this.'

20

I'm the Wind! I am strong!
I can blow the clouds along!
Gonna hurl that roof as high as it can be,
No one is as strong as me.

And the Wind blew a storm force 11!

(3RD WIND BLOWING MUSIC, *f*)

'Impressive,' admitted the Sun. 'But watch this.'

It's holiday time for everyone again,
Time to swim and jump and run again,
Take your clothes off, here's the sun
again,
Summer has begun again! It's fun again!

And the Sun shone 50 degrees frying pan!

(3RD SUN SHINING MUSIC, *f*)

And then the Sun and the Wind really went for each other!

(Sing the Wind's and Sun's third verses as partner songs. Alternatively, sing them one after another; start quietly and end loudly.)

'This is getting us nowhere,' said the Wind.

'You're right,' agreed the Sun. 'What we need is proof.'

Just then, a traveller came walking down the road, wearing a heavy cloak.

'I'll show you,' said the Wind. 'I'll blow his cloak off.' And it blew, starting off at light air force 1 – then 2, gentle breeze force 3 – 4, 5, strong breeze force 6 – 7, gale force 8 – 9, 10 – storm force 11 – hurricane force 12!

(4TH WIND BLOWING MUSIC ——— >)

But the harder the Wind blew, the tighter the traveller wrapped his cloak around himself – and eventually, the Wind had to admit defeat.

'Right,' said the Sun. 'Quite finished? Watch this, then.' And it shone, starting lukewarm at 10 degrees celsius, then hot at 20 degrees, then baking at 30 degrees, frying at 40, burning at 50 – boiling at a world record 56 degrees!

(4TH SUN SHINING MUSIC ———)

Finally, the traveller could take no more. He unbuttoned his cloak, threw it back – then, finally, took it off!

The Sun had won – it shouted 'HOORAY!'

And all the Wind could manage to say was: 'OH BLOW!'

Short activities

The children learn the two songs. Then they perform vocal sounds with different dynamics.

Wind and Sun Songs

What you will need

* These chime bar notes

Preparation

1. Learn the three Wind verses which are sung to the melody of *This Old Man*. Then learn the three Sun verses which are sung to the melody of *Michael Finnigin*. The starting notes for the melodies are:

C' A C'
I'm the wind

C F F F F
When sum-mer-time comes

2. Make up actions to go with each verse.

3. Choose two children to play the starting notes for each verse. Then perform the Sun and the Wind verses in the order they appear in the story. At the point in the story when the Sun and the Wind really go for each other, sing the third Wind verse starting quietly and getting louder, followed by the third Sun verse performed in the same way.

Wind and Sun Sounds

What you will need

* Enlarged photocopies of the *Wind* and *Sun Scores* (page 23), and the *Dynamics Box* (page 25)

Preparation

1. Introduce the musical symbols *p*, *mf* and *f* to the children. They indicate dynamic levels and their meanings are given in the *Dynamics Box*.

2. Play the game *Different Dynamics* (page 25).

3. Ask the children to make a long whistling sound for the Wind. Each child should breathe in his/her own time so that the overall sound is continuous. Do the same with a sizzling sound for the sun.

4. Perform the sound effects at different dynamic levels – first *p*, then *mf* and finally *f*. Make sure the children achieve contrast between each dynamic level.

5. Introduce the musical terms crescendo and diminuendo (see the *Dynamics Box*).

6. Ask the children to make whistling sounds with a crescendo and diminuendo. To indicate to the children to get louder or quieter, either:
• move a ruler across the *Wind Score*;
• use arm movements (as in *Different Dynamics*);
• slowly read the section of the story which relates to the gradual increase in wind force.

The children begin very quietly at force 1. On reaching force 12, their loud sound gets quieter and stops as the hurricane quickly dies away.

7. Do the same with the *Sun Score*. However, instead of ending with a diminuendo, cue the children to shout *Bang!* as the thermometer explodes. The children should practise shouting together as one loud voice.

Performance

At the appropriate moments as you read the story, the children sing the Wind and Sun verses and perform the sound effects with the indicated dynamics.

Wind Score for 4th Wind Blowing Music featuring crescendo and diminuendo (Beaufort scale)

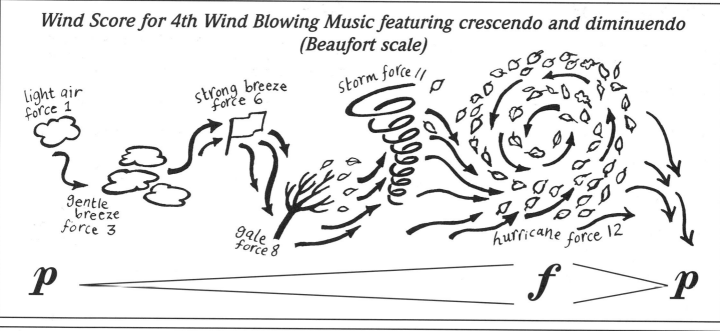

light air force 1

gentle breeze force 3

strong breeze force 6

gale force 8

storm force 11

hurricane force 12

p   *f*   *p*

Sun Score for 4th Sun Shining Music featuring crescendo (Celsius scale)

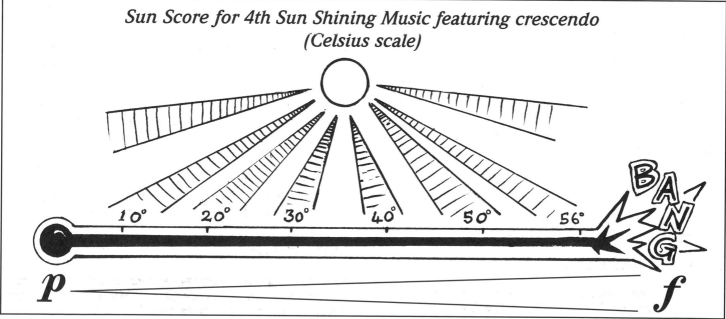

10° 20° 30° 40° 50° 56°

BANG

p   *f*

Longer activities

The children sing the Wind and Sun songs as partner songs. (Partner songs are songs that fit together when sung at the same time.) They then perform instrumental sounds at various dynamics to make *Wind* and *Sun Music*.

Wind and Sun Partner Songs

What you will need

* These chime bars notes

Preparation

Divide the children into two groups – one to sing the Wind song, the other the Sun song (final verses only). Choose a child from each group to play the starting notes for its song.

In order that the songs fit together when sung simultaneously, the Sun group must start first. The Wind group start on the Sun group's *sum-*. The beginnings of the songs fit together like this:

	C'	A	C'
	I'm	the	wind
C	F	F F	F
When	sum-mer-time		comes

Wind music

What you will need

* Photocopies of the *Wind and Sun Scores* (page 23)
* A selection of tuned and untuned percussion, wind instruments and 'junk' sound sources

Preparation

1. Divide the class into six groups, one for each wind force shown on the *Wind Score*.

2. Ask the children in each group to suggest instrumental or 'junk' sounds that would be suitable for their strength of wind force. Look at the pictures on the *Wind Score* for ideas. Here are some examples:

 blow gently across a tube or bottle for *light air force 1*

 rustle or scrunch paper for *gentle breeze force 3*

 flap material or wobble stiff card for *strong breeze force 6*

 play creaking or snapping branch sounds on a scraper for *gale force 8*

 blow whistles or swing whirly tubes for *storm force 11*

 play swirly patterns on several xylophones for *hurricane force 12*

3. Choose children in each group to perform on instruments as you read the part of the story relating to the *Wind Score*. As the children hear their wind force strength called out, they join in and gradually get louder. They can either make continuous sounds, improvise freely, or play a repeating word rhythm e.g. *I'm the wind!* The other children can make the vocal whistling sound. Gradually the music builds up to hurricane force 12, then fades away. Repeat the activity to give other children a turn at playing the instruments.

Sun Music

What you will need

* Six chime bars of
different pitches, e.g.
* A cymbal and a drum

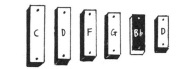

Choose one child (the sun) to play a continuous roll on
suspended cymbal. Then, give one chime bar to each of
the six groups from a rising set of six notes to
represent the six degrees of temperature, e.g.

group: 10°   20°   30°   40°   50°   56°

One child in each group plays a continuous sound on
their chime bar by tapping it quickly. The other
children in the group make sizzling sounds, or sing
their note with a sizzling or buzzing sound. The groups
join in one by one and gradually get louder. On
reaching boiling point, make a loud bang on a drum for
the exploding thermometer. This acts as a signal for
everyone suddenly to stop playing and singing.

Performance

Divide the class into two groups – Sun and Wind
groups. Subdivide the Wind group into the six wind
force groups and sit them in the order they perform in
the cue score ready with their instruments. Do the
same with the Sun group. Choose individual groups to
play their instruments for the 1st, 2nd and 3rd *Wind
Blowing* and *Sun Shining* music made after each verse.

For the *4th Wind Blowing* music, you can write the
increments of wind force strength on to separate pieces
of card for the narrator to hold up in turn show the
increase in wind force. For the *4th Sun Shining* music,
draw a large thermometer and point at it to indicate
the rising temperature.

Dynamics Box

symbol	Italian term	pronunciation	meaning
p	*piano*	pee-<u>ah</u>-no	quiet
mf	*mezzo forte*	<u>met</u>-so <u>for</u>-tay	moderately loud
f	*forte*	<u>for</u>-tay	loud
<	*crescendo*	cresh-<u>en</u>-doh	becoming louder
>	*diminuendo*	dim-in-yu-<u>en</u>-do	becoming quieter

Different Dynamics

Draw the dynamic symbols *p*, *mf* and *f* on
separate pieces of card (each approximately 10cm x
10cm).

Hold the cards together with one card showing for
the children to see. Then ask the class to sing either
the *Wind song* or the *Sun song* at the dynamic level
shown on the card. At the end of the first line of the
song show a different card. The class (without
pausing) sing the next line of the song at the dynamic
shown and so on.
• To make the game easier, change the cards at the
end of every two lines.
• To make it harder, change the cards more
frequently and less predictably.
• To make a longer game, repeat the song several
times.

Play the game with a conductor instead of cards. The
conductor shows the three dynamic levels with two
hands – near together, apart and far apart. (If you
wish, the conductor can also show crescendos and
diminuendos by gradually widening or narrowing the
distance between the two hands.)

Henry VIII's Proposal

This song, which is sung to the tune of *Widdicombe Fair*, is a conversation between Henry VIII and a fictional pretty, young maid. In it, the six wives of Henry VIII are listed in the order in which they married him. The children learn the song and play an untuned ostinato accompaniment (short activities). They then learn a circle dance (longer activity).

Henry:
Oh maid, fair maid, please marry me do!
Henery, Henery, Henry's my name.
I'm King of all England, and I fancy you!
    You will live in a palace,
    Sipping cider from a chalice,
    What a future! What a life!
Oh, tell me that you'll be my wife!
Oh, tell me that you'll be my wife!

Henry:
Oh maid, fair maid, if you'll marry me,
Henery, Henery, Henry am I,
A dutiful husband I swear I will be,
    I'll surprise you with presents,
    Yellow roses, brace of pheasants,
    And flasks of sweet wine,
Oh, tell me that you will be mine,
Oh, tell me that you will be mine!

Maid:
Oh sire, good sire, you'll not take me in,
Henery, Henery, I know your game!
First Catherine of Aragon, then Anne Boleyn,
    Jane Seymour, Anne of Cleves,
    Catherine Howard, Catherine Parr,
    All those wives, sire, what a lot!
So marry you, sire, I will not,
So marry you, sire, I will not.

Maid:
Oh sire, good sire, I bid you good day,
Henery, Henery, Henry, you lie!
Your bad reputation will not go away,
    With divorces and weddings
    Not to mention beheadings,
    Or so it is said;
I'm really quite fond of my head,
I'd rather stay single instead!

Short activities

The children sing the song and perform an accompaniment.

The song

Teach the children the song. It is sung to the tune of *Widdicombe Fair*. Divide into two groups: one sings Henry's verses, the other the maid's.

Ostinato accompaniment

What you will need

* A selection of untuned instruments

Preparation

1. Ask some children to clap or tap the rhythm of the words *Oh maid, fair maid* as an ostinato while the others sing one of Henry's verses.

2. Ask some different children to clap or tap the rhythm of the words *You'll not take me in* as an ostinato while the others sing one of the maid's verses.

3. Talk about the different sound qualities of the untuned percussion instruments you have available. Choose instruments which would be appropriate for Henry. Find contrasting instruments for the maid.

4. Choose children to play the *Oh maid, fair maid* rhythm on Henry's instruments throughout his verses. Choose other children to play the *You'll not take me in* rhythm on the maid's instruments throughout her verses. Perform the whole song with the instrumental ostinatos.

Longer activity

The children learn a circle dance.

Circle dance

1. Make two circles – an outer circle to sing Henry's verses and an inner circle to sing the maid's. The children in each circle hold hands at shoulder height.

2. Practise moving clockwise round the circle with this step-slide move which lasts for two counts: step with the left foot, then slide the right foot.

Do this six times. Then wait for six counts. Repeat the step-slide move four times. This sequence of moves lasts the length of a verse.

3. Repeat stage 2, moving anti-clockwise. Step with the right foot and slide the left foot.

4. Perform the circle dance with the song. When the outer circle sings Henry's verses, the inner circle moves clockwise. When the inner circle sings the maid's verses, the outer circle moves anti-clockwise.

The Princess and the Pea

This is a rap with a steady pulse. The children tap the beat and explore rapping techniques (short activities) and develop a rhythmic accompaniment using accents and instruments (longer activity).

'Son,' said the King, 'Gotta find yourself a wife!
You can't stay single for the rest of your life.'
'Right,' said the Prince, 'Guess I'd better say
    YES –
But only if I find myself a real Princess.'

    A real Princess, a real Princess,
    The Prince has gotta find himself
    A real Princess.

When the word got around, shoulda seen the
    volunteers,
Tall ones, short ones, ones with funny ears,
One played the trumpet,
    another played the pipe,
'Sorry,' said the Prince,
    'but they're not my type,

    I want a real Princess, a real Princess.'
    The Prince has gotta find himself
    A real Princess.

One dark night, when the winds did roar,
Came a-knock, knock, knocking
    on the castle door!
'Help!' said a voice,
    'I've lost my way,
And I've come here looking
    for a place to stay.

    I'm a real Princess, a real Princess,
    Please let me in, 'cause I'm
    A real Princess.'

'Right,' said the Queen, 'We'll put it to the
test.
Come right in, dear, be our guest.
Don't forget your manners, Son,
see she's warm and fed.
Excuse me for a minute while I organise her
bed.'

She's a real Princess? A real Princess?
I wonder if it's true that she's
A real Princess?

One fat mattress, another on the top,
Another, then another, but we still won't stop,
Pile those duvets high as they can be!
And right at the bottom, put a little bitty pea.

A real Princess, a real Princess,
We'll soon find out if she's
A real Princess.

The girl climbed the ladder and she lay right
down,
'Ooh!' she said, and she gave a little frown,
'There's something in the bed, and it's
digging in deep,
I can't stay here, 'cause I'll never get to sleep.'

She's a real Princess! A real Princess!
That only goes to prove that she's
A real Princess!

The end of the tale isn't very hard to guess,
The prince got married to the real Princess,
Now they're together and as happy as can be,
And the names of their children all begin with
a P!

A real Princess, a real Princess,
At last the Prince has found himself
A real Princess!

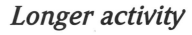

Short activities

The children perform the rap while keeping a steady beat. Then they emphasize different beats and words by making them louder (accent) or by changing the sound quality (timbre).

1. Read the first verse of the rap to the children taking care to emphasize the pulse with your voice:

'Son,' said the king, 'Got-ta find yourself a wife!'

2. Lightly pat the same beat on your knees and get everyone to join in. When everyone is patting together, all chant the first verse of the rap. (If the children find it difficult to pat the beat and chant the rap at the same time, divide into two groups – one group patting, the other group rapping. Then, when the children are more confident, revert back to patting and rapping as one group.) Repeat this activity for all the verses.

3. Ask the children to add two claps on the word *princess* whenever it appears in the rap.

4. Try out this rap technique. Divide the lines of the rap between individuals or small groups. Everyone else joins in on selected words or phrases to give them greater emphasis. In the example below, everyone can join in on the underlined words.

 'Son,' said the king,
    'Gotta find yourself a wife!
You can't stay single for the rest of your life.'

 'Right,' said the prince,
    'Guess I'd better say yes –
But only if I find myself a real princess.

 A real princess, a real princess,
The prince has gotta find himself
A real princess.'

30

Longer activity

The children explore instrumental sounds. They develop further the skill of maintaining a steady beat and emphasizing individual beats when they make up an instrumental accompaniment for the rap.

What you will need

* A selection of nine instruments, one for each of two special effects, and one for each of the seven verses, e.g.

 pea-pod instrument, e.g. a gato drum to tap, or a container filled with dried peas

 princess; a 'delicate' sounding instrument to play the word rhythm, e.g. triangle

 verse 1; royal-sounding instrument, e.g. cymbals

 verse 2; wind sounds for the trumpet or pipe, e.g. kazoo, recorder, whistle

 verse 3; wooden door knocking sounds, e.g. wood block

 verse 4; springing sounds for the bed springs, e.g. rubber bands, vibraslaps

 verse 5; heavy, dull sounds for the mattress piling, e.g. drum

 verse 6; wooden ladder sounds, e.g. guiro, xylophone

verse 7; metal ringing sounds for wedding bells, e.g. chime bars playing C' B A G F E D C

Preparation

1. Play the *Eight Beats Number Game.*

2. Accompany the rap with a count of eight beats. Divide the children into two groups: group 1 repeats a count of eight steady beats while group 2 chants a verse of the rap. Ask the children on which numbers is the word *princess* spoken. (2 and 3, 6 and 7).

A real	*prin - cess,*		a real	*prin - cess ...*	
1	2	3	4	5	6	7	8

How many counts of eight does it take to rap a verse? (Six.)

Repeat the count of eight with the rap.

3. Choose one child to accompany the chorus (*A real princess ...*) by playing a steady beat on a *pea-pod* sounding instrument (e.g. gato drum). Choose another child to play the word rhythm *princess* whenever it appears in the rap on a 'delicate' sounding instrument, (e.g. triangle).

4. Talk about the sounds that are suggested in each verse and find instruments that make similar sounds.

Choose a player for each *verse* instrument. In turn, rap each verse and ask the corresponding player to join in by playing on some or all of the beats in the first half of the verse. In the example below, a wood block plays knocking sounds.

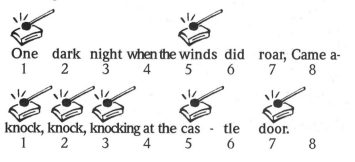

One	dark	night	when the	winds	did	roar, Came a-
1	2	3	4	5	6	7	8

knock,	knock,	knocking	at the	cas -	tle	door.
1	2	3	4	5	6	7	8

Performance

Choose two children to play the *pea-pod* and *princess* sounds to accompany the rap. Seven more volunteers play the instruments chosen for each verse. Play eight beats of *pea-pod* sounds for an introduction and between each verse to give the rappers a break.

Further development

Making a score
A score gives a visual reminder of how the sounds and players are organised. To make a score, enlarge a copy of the words of each verse of the rap and let each group design their own score. They can:
• write the rappers names against each line or verse;
• underline the words which are said by everyone (rap technique – short activity);
• draw a picture or symbol to show the instruments used for each verse;
• show each verse instrument's pattern of beats by either writing sound effect symbols above the words or by circling sets of numbers, e.g:

Eight Beats Number Game

The children sit in a circle. Choose a leader. The leader counts up to eight beats and claps on several numbers (e.g. 1 3 4 7 8). Without a break, at the end of the leader's count of eight, the class begin counting and copy the leader's 'pattern' of beats.

The game repeats with a new leader – the next child in the circle. Continue, if possible, without a gap. (If the children find it difficult to remember the leader's pattern of beats, ask each leader to clap on only two or three numbers.)

Rumpelstiltskin

The story is told in narrative and song (sung to the tune of *Oranges and Lemons*). The children play a name game (short activity), play a song accompaniment and make up music representing straw being turned into gold (longer activities).

The miller was very proud of Martha, his daughter – so proud that he couldn't stop boasting about her. 'She's very clever, you know,' he said. 'Why, she can even spin straw into gold.'

The story spread, as tales do, and at last the King heard about the miller's claim and decided to see for himself whether or not it was true. He took Martha to a high tower, where they climbed a great number of steps. At the very top was a room with a squeaky door, which was piled to the ceiling with straw. The King gave her a spinning wheel and said, 'Right, off you go. Get this lot spun into gold by tomorrow morning, or you and your dad will be in serious trouble.' Poor Martha. She had no idea how to make gold from straw. Once she was alone, she burst into tears.

All at once, there was a loud bang and a flash of light and there before her stood a strange little man who swept off his hat, bowed low, and said, 'Now, what's all this about, young lady? Why are you crying?'

'I have to spin all this straw into gold,' sobbed Martha, 'and I don't know how.'

'Spin straw into gold?' shouted the little man. 'Is that all? Nothing to it!' And he jumped on to a bale of straw and sang (to the tune of *Oranges and Lemons*):

I can spin moonbeams
And I can spin rainbows,
Whatever you bring me
I am able to spin.
   I'll spin the straw
   For your pretty green necklace,
   Pass me that wheel,
   And I'll gladly begin.
I can spin moonbeams
And I can spin rainbows,
Whatever you bring me
I am able to spin.

Martha agreed to give him her necklace – and at once the little man sat himself at the wheel and began to spin. As the wheel turned, before her very eyes, the spool filled with spun gold.

(1ST STRAW INTO GOLD MUSIC)

Throughout the night, the piles of straw shrank and the spools of gold rose. When at last the straw was all gone, the little man rose, bowed, snatched Martha's green necklace – and vanished!

The King could hardly believe his eyes when he saw all that gold. But he wanted more. He took Martha to an even higher tower, with many more steps and an even squeakier door leading into an even bigger room filled with even more straw. Again, the King ordered her to spin it into gold. Again, as soon as he had gone, she burst into tears. Again there was a bang and a flash and, again, the little man appeared and sang:

I can spin moonbeams
And I can spin rainbows,
Whatever you bring me
I am able to spin.
   I'll spin the straw
   For the ring on your finger,
   Pass me that wheel,
   And I'll gladly begin.
I can spin moonbeams
And I can spin rainbows,
Whatever you bring me
I am able to spin.

Martha agreed, the little man sat down and began to spin and the same thing happened as before.

(2ND STRAW INTO GOLD MUSIC)

At last the straw was all gone, the little man bowed, snatched the ring – and vanished.

But the King still wasn't satisfied. He took Martha to the highest tower of all – the one with hundreds of steps and the squeakiest door of the lot, leading into a huge room simply bursting with straw. 'Spin all this by morning, Martha,' said the King, 'and I'll marry you.'

That made her cry more than ever. But then there was a bang and a flash ... and there was the little man, for the third time running. Martha wondered what he would ask for as payment – for she had nothing left to give him. And he sang:

I can spin moonbeams
And I can spin rainbows,
Whatever you bring me
I am able to spin.
   I'll spin the straw,
   But the price is your baby,
   Pass me the wheel,
   And I'll gladly begin.
I can spin moonbeams ...

'I don't understand,' said Martha.

'It's simple,' said the little man. 'If I'm to help you, I'll take your first born child as payment.'

Poor Martha had to agree. Once again, he sat at the wheel and spun all the straw into gold.

(3RD STRAW INTO GOLD MUSIC)

Next morning, the King was so thrilled to see all that gold that he did indeed marry her – and Martha, the miller's daughter, became Queen of the land.

A year later, she gave birth to a fine baby boy. By this time she had forgotten all about the little man, until one evening, when she was alone, there was a bang and a flash and there he stood.

'Here I am again,' he said. 'I've come for what you promised me.'

Martha was terrified. She cried as though her heart would break. The little man felt rather sorry for her. 'Tell you what. I'll give you a chance. If, in three days, you can discover what my name is, you can keep the child!' And he vanished.

Martha spent the whole night writing out lists of all the names she had ever heard of.

The next night, the little man returned. And this is what he said:

(1ST NAME GAME CHANT)

Got your little list?
Wanna play the game?
Ready? Steady?
What's my name?

>   **Sam!**
>   **No! That's not my name!**
>   **Mohammed!**
>   **No! That's not my name!**
>   **David!**
>   **No! That's not my name!**
>   **Nigel!**
>   **No! That's not my name!**

(Continue with more names then chant final verse:)

You didn't get the name right,
That's a shame,
Better luck next time,
End of game!

And he vanished.

Desperately, Queen Martha sent out messengers to make enquiries about any other names she may have forgotten or not heard of. When the little man appeared that

night, she tried again.

(2ND NAME GAME CHANT)

Got your little list? ...

Freddy!
No! That's not my name! ...

(Continue with more names then chant final verse.)

On the third day, the messengers returned to report that they had found no new names. But one of them had some news.

'As I came to a great mountain beyond the forest,' he said, 'I saw a little man dancing around a fire, singing a strange song. It went like this':

I can spin moonbeams
And I can spin rainbows,
Whatever you bring me
I am able to spin.
   Soon I will spin me,
   The laugh of a baby,
   Sure as my birth name
   Is Rumpelstiltskin.
I can spin moonbeams
And I can spin rainbows,
Whatever you bring me
I am able to spin.

You can imagine the Queen's relief! That evening, when the little man appeared again and asked her what his name was, the Queen replied:

(All shout): RUMPELSTILTSKIN!

And at this, the little man gave a cry of rage and stamped his foot so hard that he sank right down into the earth. He was never seen again. Although sometimes, on windy nights, as she sits rocking the cradle, Queen Martha thinks she can hear faraway singing:

I can spin moonbeams ...

Rumpelstiltskin – musical development

Short activity

The children learn the song and play the name game.

1. Teach the children the song. Notice that each verse has three sections – the third is a repeat of the first.

2. In the story, Queen Martha has to find out Rumpelstiltskin's name. Ask the children to think of names.

3. Together, clap a steady beat and chant:

Got your little list? Wanna play the game?

Rea-dy? Stea-dy? What's my name?

4. Keep the handclap going and point to individual children who shout out names they have thought of followed by the class response, e.g:

Sam! No! That's not my name!

Ab-dul! No! That's not my name!

Ka-tie! No! That's not my name!

Wayne! No! That's not my name!
(and so on)

5. When everyone's had a turn (or, when someone gets stuck), end with the final verse:

You did-n't get the name right, That's a shame,

Bet-ter luck next time, End of game!

Longer activities

The children play a song accompaniment and compose *Straw into Gold Music*.

Song Accompaniment

The children perform a *knees-clap-clap* action pattern and accompany the song using notes played on tuned percussion and/or keyboards.

What you will need

* Any tuned percussion instruments (e.g. chime bars, xylophones, glockenspiels) with these notes, and/or keyboards
* Enlarged photocopies of the *Spinning Wheel Score* (page 37)

Preparation

1. Begin by teaching the children the *knees-clap-clap* pattern:

Ask them to repeat it continuously with a steady beat.

2. The song can be sung with the *knees-clap-clap* pattern. (The first two lines of the song are shown with the pattern on page 37.) The song is in three sections. For each section, the pattern is performed eight times.

Divide the children into two groups – one to perform the *knees-clap-clap* pattern, the other to sing the song.

3. Show the children the *Spinning Wheel Score*. The wheel has eight spokes – one for the beginning of each *knees-clap-clap* pattern shown on the outside.

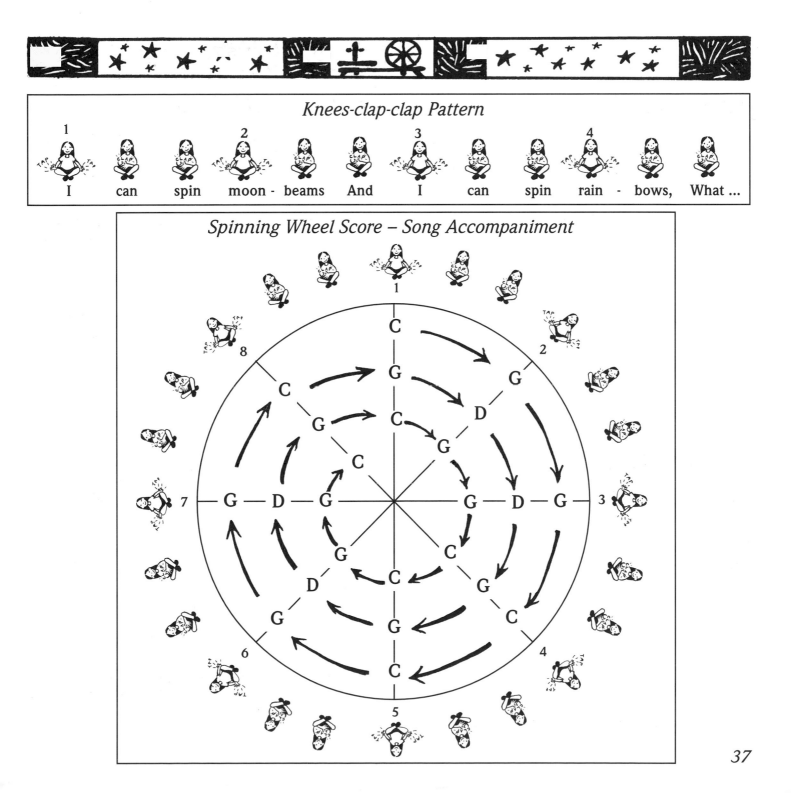

Knees-clap-clap Pattern

1 I can spin 2 moon - beams And 3 I can spin 4 rain - bows, What ...

Spinning Wheel Score – Song Accompaniment

37

Ask the children to accompany the song by playing the notes inside the *Spinning Wheel Score*. They read the notes one at a time, beginning at 1, then follow the arrows spiralling inwards.

4. To perform the song with the accompaniment, divide the children into three groups:
• one group sings the song;
• one group performs the *knees-clap-clap* pattern and counts from 1 to 8 three times (once for each section of the song);
• one group plays the tuned accompaniment; the players must sound each note as the numbers progress around the wheel.

Straw into Gold Music

The children compose music to represent the straw changing into gold. The tuned instruments suggest the motion of the *Spinning Wheel*, and the untuned and 'junk' instruments suggest the qualities of straw and gold.

What you will need

* Tuned instruments (e.g. chime bars, glockenspiels, xylophones, keyboards) to suggest the *spinning* sounds
* Untuned and 'junk' instruments to suggest *straw*, e.g.

* Untuned and 'junk' instruments to suggest *gold*, e.g.

Preparation

1. Begin by making up music to suggest the motion of the spinning wheel. For this, the children will need tuned instruments.

The children think of words about or suggesting the motion of the spinning wheel (e.g. *wheel keeps turning; winding, twisting, turning; spinning straw*). They then make up *spinning wheel patterns* out of notes to suggest regular, fast-moving spinning sounds. Here are some example spinning wheel patterns:

fast pattern	D	C	D	C	D	C
	wind - ing,	twist - ing,	turn - ing ...			

slow pattern	C	C	A
	spin -	ning	straw ...

fast and slow	G	A	G	A
pattern	wheel keeps turn	-	ing ...	

They are repeated over and over again.

2. Ask the children to decide how many times each spinning wheel pattern is played and how the patterns should be organised into a piece (e.g. begin with a slower pattern, then add faster patterns). Children can share instruments to play several patterns.

3. Prepare to make *Straw into Gold Music*. Begin by playing the game *Clap Overlap* on page 39.

4. Ask the children to explore which untuned instruments make sounds that suggest straw and gold. Organise the sounds into two groups – a *straw* group and a *gold* group.

5. Choose two players to perform the *Straw into Gold example score* on page 39. One plays a *straw*

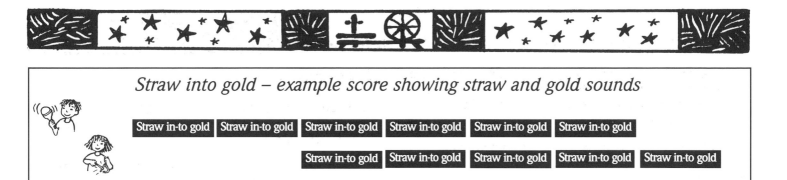

Straw into gold – example score showing straw and gold sounds

Straw in-to gold	Straw in-to gold	Straw in-to gold	Straw in-to gold	Straw in-to gold	Straw in-to gold
	Straw in-to gold	Straw in-to gold	Straw in-to gold	Straw in-to gold	Straw in-to gold

instrument (e.g. shaker), the other a *gold* instrument (e.g. triangle). The *straw* player begins by tapping the rhythm of the words *straw into gold* on the shaker. After playing this twice, the *gold* player joins in. They play together four times, before the *straw* player drops out, leaving the *gold* player playing once before finishing.

6. Ask pairs of children to make up their own *Straw into Gold Scores*. They choose a word rhythm and instruments. They begin with straw sounds, end with gold sounds, and must decide when their straw turns into gold.

7. The children organise their *Straw into Gold* performance. They can choose to:
• have several pairs performing their straw into gold score either simultaneously, or one after another;
• perform the spinning sounds before, after, or at the same time as the straw into gold sounds.

Performance

Incorporate the *Name Game*, song and accompaniment and *Straw into Gold Music* into a performance of the story.

Clap Overlap

In this game, the children explore overlapping sounds.

Make fast clapping sounds (this need not be in any rhythm) and create overlapping sounds:

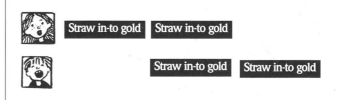

Repeat this with different body sounds (e.g. patting knees, rubbing hands), with vocal sounds (e.g. humming) and word rhythms, e.g:

Straw in-to gold	Straw in-to gold
Straw in-to gold	Straw in-to gold

Stone Soup

This story is told in narrative and song, (sung to the tune of *The Hokey Cokey*). The children accompany the song with a repeating rhythm (ostinato) and actions (short activities). Then they build up layers of rhythms to make textures (longer activity).

One winter's night, a tramp knocked at a cottage door and asked for shelter. 'Oh, all right,' grumbled the old woman who lived there. 'But don't expect me to feed you. I haven't a thing in the house.'

'No? Well, in that case, you're in luck,' said the tramp, taking a stone from his pocket. 'See this? It makes the best stone soup you've ever tasted.'

'Stone soup?' said the old woman.

'Stone soup,' nodded the tramp, and he sang (to the tune of *The Hokey Cokey*):

You take a small, round stone,
You pop it in the pot,
You add a lot of water
And you make it nice and hot,
Then you serve it in a basin
With a ladle or a scoop,
That's how you make stone soup!
    Oooh, missus, it's delicious,
    Oooh, missus, it's nutritious,
    Stop looking so suspicious,
    Wait 'til you try my hot stone soup!

'That's a new one on me,' said the woman. 'Just hot water, you say?'

'That's right,' nodded the tramp.

So the old woman set a pan full of water on the fire to heat – and the tramp dropped in the stone. Then they sat back to wait. After a while, the tramp said 'I've just thought. Last time I made this, I added salt and pepper. It makes an ordinary soup into a good soup.' And he sang:

You take a small, round stone,
You pop it in the pot,
Add a little salt and pepper,
They're the things that I forgot!
Then you serve it in a basin
With a ladle or a scoop,
That's how you make stone soup!
    Oooh, missus, it's delicious,
    Oooh, missus, it's nutritious,
    Stop looking so suspicious,
    Wait 'til you try my hot stone soup!

So the old woman went to her cupboard, fetched the salt and pepper and put some into the water. After a few more minutes, she looked in the pot. And the tramp said 'You know, it's a pity you don't have a potato. A single potato would make a good soup into very good soup.' And he sang:

You take a small, round stone,
You pop it in the pot,
You add a big potato,
That's the thing that I forgot!
Then you serve it in a basin
With a ladle or a scoop,
That's how you make stone soup!
    Oooh, missus, it's delicious,
    Oooh, missus, it's nutritious,
    Stop looking so suspicious,
    Wait 'til you try my hot stone soup!

'Hmm. I just might have one of those,' said the old woman, and off she bustled to get one. She peeled it, chopped it, and added it to the soup. Then again, they waited.

After a bit, the tramp said 'I've just remembered! I always add an onion and a carrot. That makes very good soup exceedingly good.' And he sang:

You take a small, round stone,
You pop it in the pot,
Add an onion and a carrot,
They're the things that I forgot,
Then you serve it in a basin
With a ladle or a scoop,
That's how you make stone soup!
    Oooh, missus, it's delicious,
    Oooh, missus, it's nutritious,
    Stop looking so suspicious,
    Wait 'til you try my hot stone soup!

Off went the woman, and returned with an onion and a carrot, which she chopped up and added to the soup. Then they sat and waited.

'Tell you what,' said the tramp after a bit. 'There's one more thing we need to make an exceedingly good soup unbelievably good.'

And he sang:

> You take a small, round stone,
> You pop it in the pot,
> You add a chunk of meat,
> That's the thing that I forgot,
> Then you serve it in a basin
> With a ladle or a scoop,
> That's how you make stone soup!
>> Oooh, missus, it's delicious,
>> Oooh, missus, it's nutritious,
>> Stop looking so suspicious,
>> Wait 'til you try my hot stone soup!

The old woman rushed to the larder and came back with a huge steak, which she chopped up and popped in the pot. By now, the soup was beginning to smell delicious.

'Time you laid the table, I think,' said the tramp. So the old woman got out her best tablecloth and china soup bowls and her best silver spoons and laid the table. And she added a loaf of bread and a bottle of wine and two glasses. Then they sat down at the table and had an absolute feast.

> You take a small, round stone,
> You pop it in the pot,
> Add a bit of this and that,
> And you wait until it's hot,
> Then you serve it in a basin
> With a ladle or a scoop,
> That's how you make stone soup!
>> Oooh, missus, it's delicious,
>> Oooh, missus, it's nutritious,
>> Stop looking so suspicious,
>> Glad we could eat my hot stone soup!

Short activities

The children accompany the song with a repeating rhythm (ostinato) and make up actions.

1. Teach the children to sing the song. It begins on the note D.

2. Ask the children to clap the *Hot stone soup* rhythm:

Hot stone soup (rest) Hot stone soup (rest)

Divide the children into two groups: one sings the song while the other accompanies it by clapping the *Hot stone soup* rhythm over and over again.

3. Ask the children to think up actions to perform with the first six lines of each verse (e.g. patting fist in palm, pointing hand down, pouring a kettle, wafting steam, holding and shaking a basin, scooping out).

4. Perform the actions in order to the *Hot stone soup* rhythm (see the box below).

Longer activity

The children work out the rhythms of word patterns, layer rhythm on rhythm to make textures and follow the directions of a conductor. The *hot stone soup* rhythm is used as a basic accompaniment throughout.

What you will need

* An enlarged copy of the *Ingredients Box* (page 44) giving the rhythms
* Several small stones or pebbles to tap together
* A selection of at least five untuned percussion instruments (e.g. claves, maracas, bongos, guiro, drum)

Preparation

1. Play the *Pass the Pebble* game (page 45).

2. Look at the *Ingredient Box*. Through discussion and demonstration find ways to chant the words in rhythms which will fit in with the beat of the song, just as *hot stone soup* does. Then choose a different body sound for each rhythm (e.g. *hot stone soup* – clap; *salt and pepper* – click fingers or pat palm with two fingers; *big potato* – pat knees; *onion and carrot* – rub hands; *chunk of meat* – tap feet).

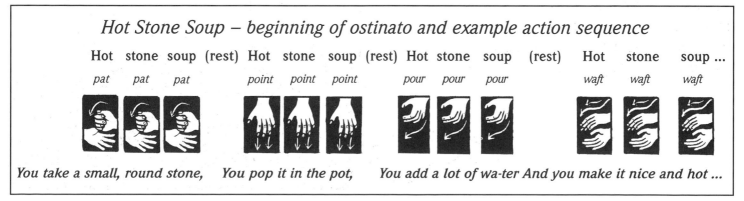

Hot Stone Soup – beginning of ostinato and example action sequence

Hot	stone	soup	(rest)	Hot	stone	soup	(rest)	Hot	stone	soup	(rest)	Hot	stone	soup ...
pat	*pat*	*pat*		*point*	*point*	*point*		*pour*	*pour*	*pour*		*waft*	*waft*	*waft*

You take a small, round stone,   *You pop it in the pot,*   *You add a lot of wa-ter And you make it nice and hot ...*

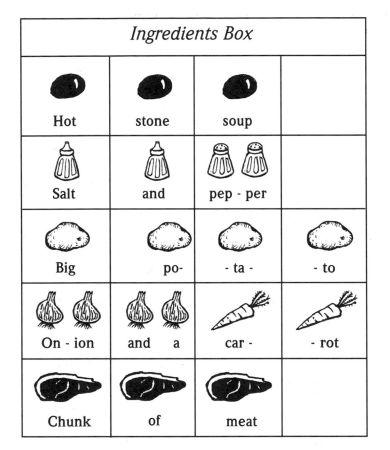

Ingredients Box			
Hot	stone	soup	
Salt	and	pep - per	
Big	po-	- ta -	- to
On - ion	and a	car -	- rot
Chunk	of	meat	

Chant and make the body sounds at the same time, repeating each rhythm several times. It may help to make 'silent beat gestures' for the empty boxes.

3. Choose volunteers to play the *hot stone soup* rhythm by tapping stones or pebbles together. Sing the first verse and chorus of the song. Accompany the chorus with the pebbles. Then, at the end, keep the pebble accompaniment going, and chant and clap the *hot stone soup* rhythm four times.

4. Combine two rhythms. Start the *hot stone soup* rhythm. Then ask the class to join in with the *salt and pepper* chant and body sound. When the children are confident, sing the second verse and chorus. At the end, chant both rhythms together as shown at the bottom of this page.

5. Repeat stage 4 for the third, fourth and fifth versions of the song, each time performing the corresponding ingredient rhythm over the pebble accompaniment.

6. Play *Chef's Secret Ingredients* (page 45).

7. Divide the class into five groups, one for each ingredient rhythm. Starting with the *hot stone soup* group, direct each group to enter one by one. The groups repeat their rhythms continuously until all groups are playing together.

Choose a conductor (the chef) to show when each group enters (the time between each entry is entirely up to the conductor). The music ends with all groups chanting and clapping the *hot stone soup* rhythm once. To indicate this, the conductor needs to make up a special signal (e.g. both hands beating three strong beats). With more experience the conductor can use other signals to stop or start individual groups and indicate changes in volume (dynamics). This will make the music more interesting and varied, but the children need to be rhythmically very secure and confident. (See the *Chef's Graphic Score* opposite – it shows an example performance.)

8. Choose untuned percussion instruments for each ingredient (e.g. salt and pepper – maracas, meat – drum, and so on). As before, the *hot stone soup* group taps stones or pebbles together.

pebbles:	hot stone soup	(rest)	hot stone soup	(rest)	hot stone soup	(rest)	hot stone soup
class:	salt and pep-per	(rest)	salt and pep-per	(rest)	salt and pep-per	(rest)	hot stone soup

Chef's Graphic Score

Hot stone soup!

Hot stone soup!

Hot stone soup!

Hot stone soup!

Hot stone soup!

Performance

Organise the children into five ingredient groups. Tell the story and sing the song with actions. At the end of each verse and chorus, the corresponding group chants and plays its rhythm with the *hot stone soup* pebble accompaniment.

At the end of the last verse and chorus, keep the pebble accompaniment going and add the rhythms as directed by the conductor. Everyone shouts *hot stone soup* to end the performance.

Chef's Secret Ingredients

A chef wants to keep the recipe for *Hot stone soup* a secret. However, everyone will be able to tell which ingredients are being used by listening to the rhythms they make.

Choose a child (the chef) to tap out the five ingredient rhythms with pebbles, one by one, in any order. After each rhythm ask the children to match the rhythm with its word pattern. Two ingredients have the same rhythm. Which ones? (*Hot stone soup* and *chunk of meat*.)

Pass the Pebble

Sit the children on the floor in a large circle and give each child a pebble.

Everyone chants the words *hot stone soup* at the same time as tapping the rhythm on the floor with pebbles. On tapping the word *soup*, the children let go of the pebbles. In the rest that follows, each child reaches in front of the child to his or her left, and picks up that pebble. The *hot stone soup* rhythm is then tapped again with the new pebble.

Keep repeating this process. The pebbles should be passed without interrupting the flow of the rhythm. Try the game slowly at first, then up to speed. Eventually replace the chanting by singing the song, but still pass the pebbles with the *hot stone soup* rhythm.

(An alternative way of organising this game is to sit the children in small groups of four or five around desks, giving each group one pebble. If you wish, you can use large erasers to avoid scratching the desks or making loud sounds.)

Mowgli in the Jungle

The story of Mowgli's journey through the jungle to find water is told with a spoken poem and a song (sung to the tune of *Down in the Valley Where Nobody Goes*). The children sing the song with actions (short activity). They also explore sounds for the hazards encountered (short activity) and make up call and response chants with instrumental accompaniments for them (longer activity).

(Poem)
Come to the jungle, if you dare.
Enemies are everywhere!
Things that bite and things that claw you,
Things that fight and things that paw you,
Things that nip you, things that scratch you,
Things that eat you when they catch you!
Come to the jungle, if you dare.
Enemies are everywhere!

(Sing to the tune of *Down in the Valley Where Nobody Goes*):

Deep in the jungle on a tropical night,
When the big, full moon is shinin' bright,
Along comes Mowgli takin' a stroll,
Headin' for the water-hole.

  Hot, hot, couldn't get no hotter,
  Hot, hot, need a drink of water,
  Yes, it's hot, hot, couldn't get no hotter,
  Coolest place is the water-hole.

Trouble is, the water-hole lies beyond the snake pit!

(SNAKE MUSIC)

Snakes didn't get him and the kid is alright,
And the big, full moon's still shinin' bright,
He's cool, he's calm, he's under control,
Headin' for the water-hole.

  Hot, hot, couldn't get no hotter,
  Hot, hot, need a drink of water,
  Yes, it's hot, hot, couldn't get no hotter,
  Coolest place is the water-hole.

Trouble is, the water-hole lies beyond the
bear cave!

(BEAR MUSIC)

Bears didn't get him and the kid is alright,
And the big, full moon's still shinin' bright,
He's cool, he's calm, he's under control,
Headin' for the water-hole.

   Hot, hot, couldn't get no hotter,
   Hot, hot, need a drink of water,
   Yes, it's hot, hot, couldn't get no hotter,
   Coolest place is the water-hole.

Trouble is, the water-hole lies beyond the tall
trees!

(TREES MUSIC)

Trees didn't get him and the kid is alright,
And the big, full moon's still shinin' bright,
He's cool, he's calm, he's under control,
Headin' for the water-hole.

Hot, hot, couldn't get no hotter,
Hot, hot, need a drink of water,
Yes, it's hot, hot, couldn't get no hotter,
Coolest place is the water-hole.

Trouble is, the water-hole lies beyond the
swamp!

(SWAMP MUSIC)

Swamp didn't get him and the kid is alright,
And the big, full moon's still shinin' bright,
And round the bend – well, bless my soul!
He's made it to the water-hole!

   Hot, hot, couldn't get no hotter,
   Hot, hot, need a drink of water,
   Yes, it's hot, hot, couldn't get no hotter,
   Coolest place is the water-hole.

(All shout:) SPLASH!

Short activities

The children learn the poem. They then learn the song with actions, and make body percussion and vocal sounds for each of the hazards encountered by Mowgli.

1. Teach the poem. (If you wish, allocate lines to individual children.) Perform the poem with a steady beat.

2. Teach the song – either with the actions suggested below or with actions invented by the children. The tune of the song is *Down in the Valley Where Nobody Goes*. It begins on the note D.

Deep in the jungle on a tropical night

clap hands with the music

When the big, full moon is shinin' bright

draw a full moon in the air

Along comes Mowgli ... the water-hole

swing arms as if walking

Hot, hot, couldn't get no hotter
fan face with hands

Hot, hot need a drink of water
pretend to drink out of a cup

Coolest place is the water hole

draw hole near the ground

Snakes didn't get him

move arm like a snake

Bears didn't get him

do a bear hug

Trees didn't get him

stretch arms and shake leaves

Swamp didn't get him

squelch through thick mud

And round the bend

alternate arms as if walking

– well, bless my soul!
put hands on hips

He's made it to the water-hole!
lift arms up in the air to celebrate!

3. Discuss the *snakes*, *bears*, *trees* and *swamp*, and ask the children to suggest vocal and body percussion sounds for each. (As the *trees* and *swamp* are habitats, the children may like to make the sounds of the animals which occupy them, e.g. bees, crocodiles.)

Practise conducting the sound effects.

4. Tell Mowgli's story starting with the poem, followed by the song with actions. Choose individual children to say the spoken links (*Trouble is ...*) and conduct the others performing the sound effects.

Longer activity

The children compose *snake*, *bears*, *trees* and *swamp* music by making up call and response chants with accompaniments.

What you will need

* Any tuned, untuned percussion, and 'junk' instruments you can make available

Preparation

1. Ask the children to imagine what Mowgli sees as he passes the snakes, bears, trees and swamp. Discuss how they look in the jungle and why they are scary to Mowgli.

2. Divide the children into four groups – one for each of the hazards encountered by Mowgli. Each group thinks of phrases to describe its hazard.

Here are some example phrases to help each group get started.
Snakes: *sssssssnakes sneaking through the grass; long, thin scaly ones; slithering and sliding.*
Bears: *big bad bears; cuff-you-round-the-head bears; take-you-unawares bears; bullying bears.*
Trees: *danger in the trees; see the bees in the trees; there's a sleepy looking cheetah; look, a cockatoo!*
Swamp: *swamp, swamp; bubbling and a-steaming; just the place for crocodiles; snap snap ouch!*

3. Each group organises phrases into a call and response chant. The group chooses one phrase for the response which will be performed by everyone (e.g. *Ssssssssnakes, sneaking through the grass*). The response alternates with different phrases performed by individuals – the calls.

Here is an example call and response for the snakes:

 Long, thin, scaly ones,
Long, thin, scaly ones,

Ssssssssssnakes!
Sneaking through the grass,

 Slithering and sliding,
And hanging from the trees,

 Ssssssssssnakes!
Sneaking through the grass,

 Poisonous ones with
Forked tongues flickering,

 Ssssssssssnakes!
Sneaking through the grass,

Ones with stripes and
Others with spots, etc

Encourage each group to perform their call and response with a steady beat.

4. Each group finds suitable instruments to accompany the group and solo lines of its call and response. The children make decisions about how and when the instruments should be played during the call and response, and who should play them.

5. Ask each group to perform its call and response with accompaniment. Ask the other groups to describe what they have heard and whether they can suggest any improvements (e.g. using voices in a more scary way, or making the words clearer).

Performance

Tell Mowgli's story, including the poem, the verses of the song with actions, the spoken links and the group call and responses with accompaniments.

Imir the Frost Giant

This Norse myth which tells of the creation of the first life form – the mighty and terrible frost giant, Imir – is told as a bard's poem. The Norsemen did not use writing until very late in their history, and so Norse myths were passed on by word of mouth. The best story-tellers were known as 'bards' and they would entertain the Lords in their halls on long, winter evenings. The bards often spoke in poetry, as this made the long stories easier to remember.

The children learn note patterns for *Imir's Call* and the regions shown in *Creation Map*. They make up accompaniments for them, and organise them into a longer piece for the end of the story.

According to the myth, there were two realms. In the north lay Niflheim; in the south lay Muspell. Between these two realms was a vast stretch of empty space known as Gin-un-ga-gap – or, Yawning Gap. Now, strange things happened between these realms – strange events that led to the creation of Imir the Frost Giant.

(IMIR'S CALL)

(Bard:)
In the beginning, there was space.
Just emptiness. Of life, no trace.
Yet, northwards lay a land of snow
Where howling winter winds did blow.

(IMIR'S CALL AND
1. HOWLING WINDS RESPONSE)

Due southward lay a land of flame
And Muspell was that region's name.
Volcanoes raged and filled the night
With tongues of flame and blinding light.

(IMIR'S CALL AND
2. VOLCANO RESPONSE)

Between the realms was empty space.
A yawning gap. A nowhere place.
In time, the Northern rivers rose.
They reached the gap, poured in, and froze!

(IMIR'S CALL AND
3. FREEZING RESPONSE)

The boiling streams of hot Muspell
Flowed to the gap and froze as well.
What happened then is strange to tell.
A wind arose in hot Muspell.

(IMIR'S CALL AND
4. HOT WIND RESPONSE)

Now, Mother Nature has a law –
'Exposed to Heat, All Ice Must Thaw'.
So winter lost its iron grip,
The ice began to melt and drip.

(IMIR'S CALL AND
5. MELTING RESPONSE)

And as the drops of water warmed
And flowed together – life was formed!
A mighty giant did appear
All made of frost. His name – Imir.

(IMIR'S CALL AND
ALL CREATION RESPONSES)

All people shudder at his name
For, with his birth, great evil came.
And many tales of him are told
Around the fires when nights are cold.
But they must wait another time
For here, my friends, I end my rhyme.

51

Imir the Frost Giant – musical development

The children explore the shapes of different note patterns on the *Creation Map*. They perform the note patterns in a call and response and make up accompaniments for them.

What you will need

* Six sets of notes:

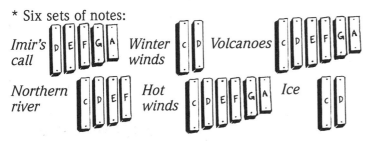

* Five enlarged photocopies of the *Creation map* (page 53)
* A selection of untuned percussion

Preparation

Melody – Call and Response

1. Choose a child to play *Imir's Call*. It's tune is the same as the beginning of *God Rest You Merry Gentlemen*, and is shown in the box below. Everyone sings the call, then rhythmically whispers the words of the first response on the *Creation Map*.

Do the same for the other four phrases on the map.

2. Ask the class to pat the drum accompaniment to *Imir's Call* (shown below) on their knees as they sing. Then choose a child to play the accompaniment on a large drum or tambour.

3. Divide the children into five groups – one for each of the regions. Allocate the notes and one phrase to each group and give them a copy of the map. The children take turns at playing the note pattern for their region. After a short period of practice, choose volunteers from each group to perform their phrase to the class.

4. The pitch shape of each note pattern is shown in the contour of the land directly below the notes on the map. Ask the class to follow the contour of the phrases as they listen to a player from each group perform again. To reinforce the shape further, encourage the class to:
• sing each note pattern back;
• show the pitch shape of each note pattern with up and down hand movements.

5. Practise the phrases as call and response. Everyone sings *Imir's Call*, then a child from one group plays its phrase as the response. Repeat the call and response. Do the same for each group in turn.

During steps 3, 4 and 5, make sure everyone has a turn at playing the note patterns.

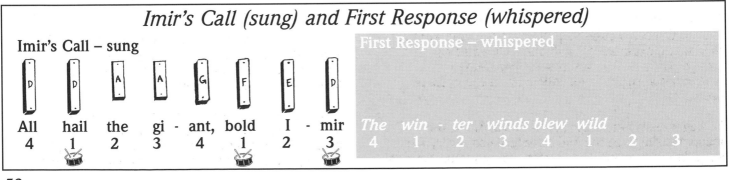

Imir's Call (sung) and First Response (whispered)

Response Accompaniments

Ask each group to find one (or more) untuned instrument with a sound quality that reflects the imagery of their phrase. One or two children in the group accompany the phrase by playing continuously throughout or just on certain words, e.g:

The winter winds blew wild

The fierce volcanoes raged

The northern rivers froze

The winds swirled hot and high

The ice did melt and drip

Performance

Choose one or more children to be bards and read the verses. Choose a child to play *Imir's Call* and another to play the drum accompaniment. Organise the five groups (with their notes and accompaniment instruments) so that they follow on in the correct order.

To begin, everyone sings *Imir's Call* without the response. Then, at the end of each verse, everyone sings *Imir's Call* and the corresponding group plays its

response phrase with accompaniment. Repeat the call and response. (It is not necessary for the children to sing the response phrases in performance, but it could be encouraged as they gain in confidence.)

At the end of the second last verse, make a long melody by performing *Imir's Call* and the five response phrases in an alternating sequence i.e. Call – phrase 1, Call – phrase 2, and so on, ending with the the call.

The Pied Piper

The story is told in song (to the tune of *Dem Bones*) and chanted rhythmic verse. (If you wish, individual lines of the chant may be spoken solo.) As they sing and chant, the children explore their vocal range and develop expression (short activities). They find tranquil sounds for the *Piper's Magical Melody* and make up a hypnotic accompaniment (longer activity). They also make up an action pattern to accompany the song, and accompaniments to the rats and kids following the piper (longer activities).

(Sing with a swing to the tune of *Dem Bones*.)
Dem rats, dem rats, dem bad rats,
Dem rats, dem rats, dem mad rats,
Dem rats, dem rats, dem bad rats,
The plague of Hamelin town.

(Chant briskly.)
Hold on to your Sunday hats!
Gonna tell you a story about some rats!
Dem big, bad rats were everywhere,
And the people of the town were in despair.
The Mayor and the Council did their best
To rid their town of the vermin pest,
But nothing seemed to do the trick,
Dem rats were smart, dem rats were quick!

Dem rats, dem rats, dem bad rats,
Dem rats, dem rats, dem mad rats,
Dem rats, dem rats, dem bad rats,
The plague of Hamelin town.

'Help!' said the Mayor, 'Can't take no more!'
Then there came a knock at the chamber door.
Into the room stepped a strange young feller
In a curious cloak of red and yeller.
'Mayor,' he said, 'you're in a spot,
If I help you out it'll cost a lot.
But if you agree to pay my fee,
I'll guarantee you'll be rat free!'

Dem rats, dem rats, dem bad rats,
Dem rats, dem rats, dem mad rats,
Dem rats, dem rats, dem bad rats,
The plague of Hamelin town.

(Chant slowly, deliberately and seriously.)
The stranger stepped into the street,
His eyes were calm, his smile was sweet.
And from his cloak a pipe he drew,
He raised it to his lips ... and blew!

(PIPER'S MAGICAL MELODY)

(Chant slowly, getting gradually faster.)
The rats looked up, the rats looked round,
Their ears pricked up, they liked the sound!
They tumbled out into the street
And danced around the Piper's feet.
Down to the river cold and grey,
The mad procession wound its way,
Enchanted by the magic sound.
The rats ran in – and all were drowned.

(Chant briskly, as at the beginning.)
'Right,' said the Piper, 'where's my fee?
Gotta gimme that gold that you promised me!'
But the Mayor and the Council turned real
    funny,
They shook their heads and they wouldn't
    pay the money.
'Hey!' said the Piper, 'That's not fair!'
Said the Mayor and the Council, 'We don't
    care!'
Then the Piper turned from the chamber
    door,
And he raised his pipe and he played once
    more.

(PIPER'S MAGICAL MELODY)

(Sing in a slow, funereal fashion.)
   All gone, all gone, they're all gone,
   All gone, all gone, they're all gone,
   All gone, all gone, they're all gone,
   They're gone from Hamelin Town.

(Chant slowly, getting gradually faster.)
The children stopped, the children heard,
They made for the street without a word.
They skipped along beneath the moon,
To the Piper's mad and magic tune.
Up on the mountain tall and steep,
A doorway leads to a cavern deep.
In ran the children, bang went the door –
And they never were heard of anymore.

(Sing slowly and sadly.)
   All gone, all gone, they're all gone,
   All gone, all gone, they're all gone,
   All gone, all gone, they're all gone,
   They're gone from Hamelin Town.

Just one small boy was left – just one.
He'd hurt his leg, he could not run.
He came back home without his friends,
And that is where the story ends.
Except, of course, you'll want to know
Wherever did the children go?
We're glad to say they found a land
Where sweets were free and rats were
   banned!

(Sing cheerfully, with a swing.)
   Dem rats, dem rats, dem bad rats,
   Dem rats, dem rats, dem mad rats,
   Dem rats, dem rats, dem bad rats,
   The plague of Hamelin town.

Short activities

The children sing the song, exploring the shape of the tune. Then they learn the chant, exploring vocal range and developing expression.

The song

1. The melody of *Dem Rats* uses three different notes, (high) B, (middle) A and (low) G. Here, they are related to three parts of the body – (high) head, (middle) belly and (low) knees.

2. Sing the song, playing the note G on a chime bar to give the starting note.

3. Make sure the children know the song well. Then ask them to sing the first half of it, patting their heads on the high notes, bellies on the middle notes and knees on the low notes. (See below for the up and down note pattern of the tune.)

4. Ask the children to work out the note and body pattern for the remaining half of the song.

5. Throughout the story, the song is sung in a variety of ways – including with a swinging beat, in a mock funereal fashion, sadly and cheerfully. To achieve contrast between each version of the song, ask the children to sing each section as directed, thinking carefully about their use of speed (tempo), volume (dynamics) and sound quality (timbre).

The chant

1. To learn the chant, perform it as a follow-my-leader:

leader:	**Hold on to your Sunday hats!**
class:	**Hold on to your Sunday hats!**
leader:	**Gonna tell you a story about some rats!**
class:	**Gonna tell you a story about some rats!**

2. Explore ways of exaggerating the vocal contour (up and down, and loud and quiet shape) of the chant for each line.

3. Choose a leader to perform a line with an exaggerated vocal contour. Repeat the follow-my-leader activity with the class copying the leader's vocal contour.

4. Perform the chant without the follow-my-leader, but try to maintain the vocal contours. (If you wish, the children may perform the whole chant together, or individuals may be allocated some lines.)

5. Finally, perform the whole story, incorporating the children's work on both the song and the chant.

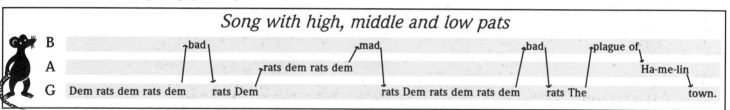
Song with high, middle and low pats

B   bad   mad   bad   plague of
A   rats dem rats dem   Ha-me-lin
G Dem rats dem rats dem   rats Dem   rats Dem rats dem rats dem   rats The   town.

Longer activities

The children find tranquil sounds suitable for the *Piper's Magical Melody* and make up a hypnotic accompaniment. They then accompany the song *Dem Rats* with patterns of body sounds. Lastly, they mirror the accumulation of *Running Rats* and *Skipping Kids* in the story by adding sounds over a walking pattern. They use this to accompany these two parts of the story.

Piper's Magical Melody

What you will need

* A selection of tuned instruments with the notes F G A B, e.g. xylophones, glockenspiels, recorders
* Metal percussion instruments, e.g. cymbals, triangles, Indian bells, wind chimes

Preparation

1. Together, gently whistle (or hum) the melody of *Dem Rats* in a tranquil, melancholy way. Then, ask volunteers to play the melody (starting on the note G) in the same way on a variety of instruments (e.g. recorder, xylophone and glockenspiel). Ask the class to decide which instrument made the most magical effect for the piper's sound. Perform the melody again by combining the whistling and chosen instrumental sound.

2. Ask volunteers to find ways of making hypnotic magical sounds on a variety of metal percussion instruments (including tuned instruments with the notes F, G, A and B). Discuss the results and ask the class to describe the effects (e.g. tingly, ringing, mesmerising, spooky). Whistle and play the melody on instruments and ask the metal percussion players to add their sounds. Some players may decide to play continuously while others drop in and out. (See the example score below.)

Song Accompaniment

Accompany the lively versions of *Dem Rats* with this pattern of body sounds. (For fun, perform the sequence with the body sounds split between three groups – one performing stamps on the first two *rats* of each line, one clapping on *dem* and one clicking on *bad/mad rats* at the end of each line.)

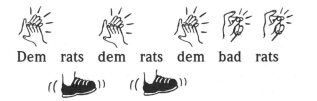

Dem rats dem rats dem bad rats

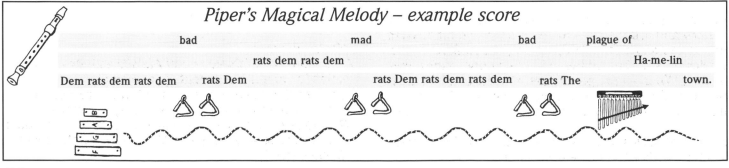

Piper's Magical Melody – example score

	bad		mad		bad	plague of
	rats dem rats dem					Ha-me-lin
Dem rats dem rats dem	rats Dem		rats Dem rats dem rats dem		rats The	town.

Running Rats and Skipping Kids

What you will need

* One or two tuned instruments with the notes F G A B
* 'Junk' instruments and scrapers that make ratty, scratching, rustling sounds, e.g. paper, chalk, brushes
* A selection of five or more untuned percussion instruments, e.g. tambourine, guiro, drum, bells

Preparation

1. Choose one or two children to play this even, steady *walking pattern* on tuned instruments:

F G A B F G A B F G A B etc

Practise chanting the verse beginning *The rats looked up* to the beat of the *walking pattern*.

2. Choose five or more children to play ratty sounds on 'junk' instruments or scrapers, for the *Running Rats*. They repeat the rhythm of the phrase *Dem rats, dem rats, dem bad rats.*

3. To the steady beat of the *walking pattern*, the children add the ratty sounds, one by one, when they feel ready. Do not direct the players, but encourage them to listen to each other carefully and to let the sounds gradually build up.

4. Put together the music as follows. Start the *walking pattern* and ask the class to chant from *The rats looked up*, up to *Piper's feet*. At this point, the *walking pattern* carries on and the children add their ratty sounds, one by one. When all the players are 'in', the children chant the second half of the verse. For dramatic effect, all instruments should stop suddenly on the word *sound*.

5. Repeat stages 3 and 4, but this time begin the ratty sounds slowly and gradually speed up.

6. To make *Skipping Kids* sounds for the verse beginning *The children stopped*, follow the procedure outlined in stages 1–5. However, use conventional percussion instruments to represent the skipping sounds. Use a different set of players from the *Running Rats*.

Performance

You do not need to include all the activities in a final performance. Select the ones you would like to incorporate according to your time and resources.

Dem Rats Song
All the children sing *Dem Rats* and accompany it with the sequence of body sounds.

Chant
This can be performed by all of the children, by small groups or by individual children.

Piper's Magical Melody
Whistle the tune and/or choose a group of children to play the melody and accompaniment on instruments.

Running Rats and Skipping Kids
Choose two groups of players and one or two children to play the walking pattern. To simplify, leave out the ratty sounds and skipping kids.

Further Development

Music corner
To extend the *Piper's Magical Melody* activity, place a variety of tuned instruments (e.g. recorder, glockenspiel, keyboard, and so on) in the corner. Let pairs of children work out how to play the melody of *Dem Rats* by ear. They can experiment playing the tune in a variety of ways (e.g. quickly, slowly, quietly, loudly, sleepily, jerkily).

Melody lines to the songs

King Midas – I Came From Alabama

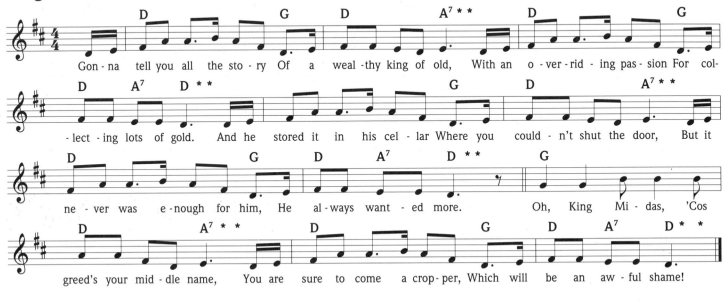

Gon - na tell you all the sto - ry Of a weal - thy king of old, With an o - ver - rid - ing pas - sion For col -
- lect - ing lots of gold. And he stored it in his cel - lar Where you could - n't shut the door, But it
ne - ver was e - nough for him, He al - ways want - ed more. Oh, King Mi - das, 'Cos
greed's your mid - dle name, You are sure to come a crop - per, Which will be an aw - ful shame!

Sleeping Beauty – On Top of Old Smokey

They say there's a cas - tle On a moun - tain so steep, In -
- side lies a prin - cess Who's for - e - ver as - leep. They
say she liked danc - ing, In a blue sa - tin gown, Then
she pricked her fin - ger, And time slowed right down.
(Getting slower)

60

The Island of Plums – *Shortnin' Bread*

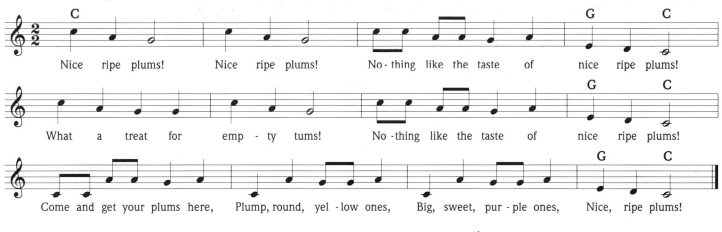

Nice ripe plums! Nice ripe plums! No-thing like the taste of nice ripe plums!

What a treat for emp-ty tums! No-thing like the taste of nice ripe plums!

Come and get your plums here, Plump, round, yel-low ones, Big, sweet, pur-ple ones, Nice, ripe plums!

The Sun and Wind

Wind Song – *This Old Man*

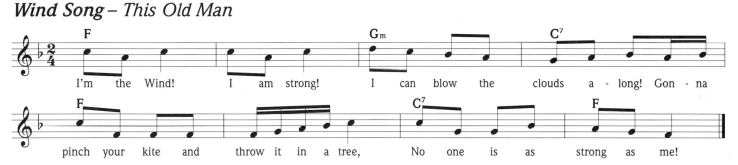

I'm the Wind! I am strong! I can blow the clouds a-long! Gon-na

pinch your kite and throw it in a tree, No one is as strong as me!

Sun Song – *Michael Finnigin*

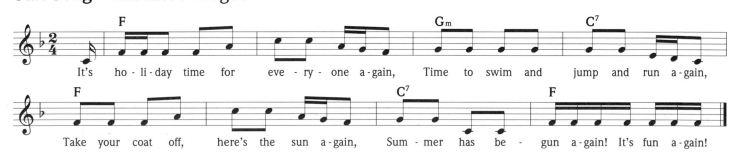

It's ho-li-day time for eve-ry-one a-gain, Time to swim and jump and run a-gain,

Take your coat off, here's the sun a-gain, Sum-mer has be-gun a-gain! It's fun a-gain!

Henry VIII's Proposal – Widdicombe Fair

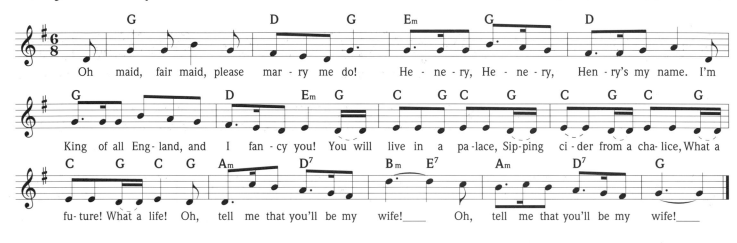

Oh maid, fair maid, please marry me do! He-ne-ry, He-ne-ry, Hen-ry's my name. I'm King of all Eng-land, and I fan-cy you! You will live in a pa-lace, Sip-ping ci-der from a cha-lice, What a fu-ture! What a life! Oh, tell me that you'll be my wife!____ Oh, tell me that you'll be my wife!____

Rumpelstiltskin – Oranges and Lemons

I can spin moon-beams and__ I can spin rain-bows, What-e-ver you bring me I am a-ble to spin. I'll spin the straw For your__ pret-ty green neck-lace, Pass me that wheel, And I'll glad-ly be-gin. I can spin moon-beams and__ I can spin rain-bows, What-e-ver you bring me I am a-ble to spin.

Stone Soup – The Hokey Cokey

You take a small, round stone, You pop it in the pot, You add a lot of wa-ter and you make it nice and hot, Then you serve it in a ba-sin With a la-dle or a scoop, That's how you make stone soup! Oooh, mis-sus, it's de-li-cious,_ Oooh, mis-sus, it's nu--tri-tious,_ Stop look-ing so sus-pi-cious,_ Wait 'til you try my hot stone soup!

Mowgli – Down in the Valley Where Nobody Goes

Deep in the jun-gle on a tro-pi-cal night,_ When the big, full moon is shin-ing bright,_ A--long comes Mow-gli, tak-in' a stroll,_ Head-in' for the wa-ter-hole._ Hot, hot, could-n't get no hot-ter,_ Hot, hot, need a drink of wa-ter, Yes, it's hot, hot, could-n't get no hot-ter, Cool-est place is the wa-ter-hole._

Imir the Frost Giant

Call – *God Rest You Merry Gentlemen*
  (beginning only)

Responses

All hail the gi - ant bold I - mir

1. The win - ter winds blew wild
2. The fierce vol - ca - noes raged
3. The nor - thern ri - vers froze
4. The winds swirled hot and high
5. The ice did melt and drip

The Pied Piper – Dem Bones

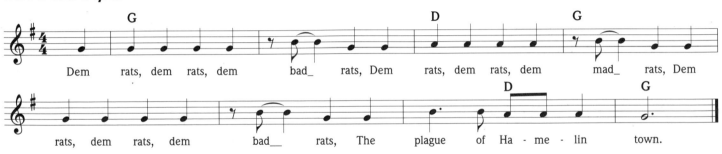

Dem rats, dem rats, dem bad_ rats, Dem rats, dem rats, dem mad_ rats, Dem

rats, dem rats, dem bad__ rats, The plague of Ha - me - lin town.